Beyond the Veil of Fate

Kevin and Marianne Nichols

Authors: Kevin and Marianne Nichols
Illustrations: Ayheka
E-mail: hopefulkevin@hotmail.com (Kevin Nichols)
Copyright: Kevin Nichols
Istanbul, Turkey, 2022
ISBN: 978-1-948575-58-4
Library of Congress Control Number: 2022945215

Beyond the Veil of Fate

Kevin and Marianne Nichols
Illustrations: Ayheka
–2022–

To my mother

Beyond the Veil
of Fate

Every baby is born naked and equal.

With her first cry, baby meets the fate awaiting her.

Fate
embraces her
unconditionally.

Like a blanket or veil she is wrapped in when she is born...

...She cannot choose the fabric, just as she cannot choose her parents or the circumstances into which she is born.

Some babies are wrapped in silky veils when they open their eyes to the world.

Some say "hello" to life with an ordinary veil.

Some are welcomed with a patched sack.

And some are
lucky to find
any cover at all.

As long as the fabric covers her body, the baby is peaceful. But what happens when she begins to outgrow it?

As time goes on, the child gets bigger, but the size of the fabric remains the same.

This begins the trials of life...

Every person is tested with the veil that wraps her when she is born.

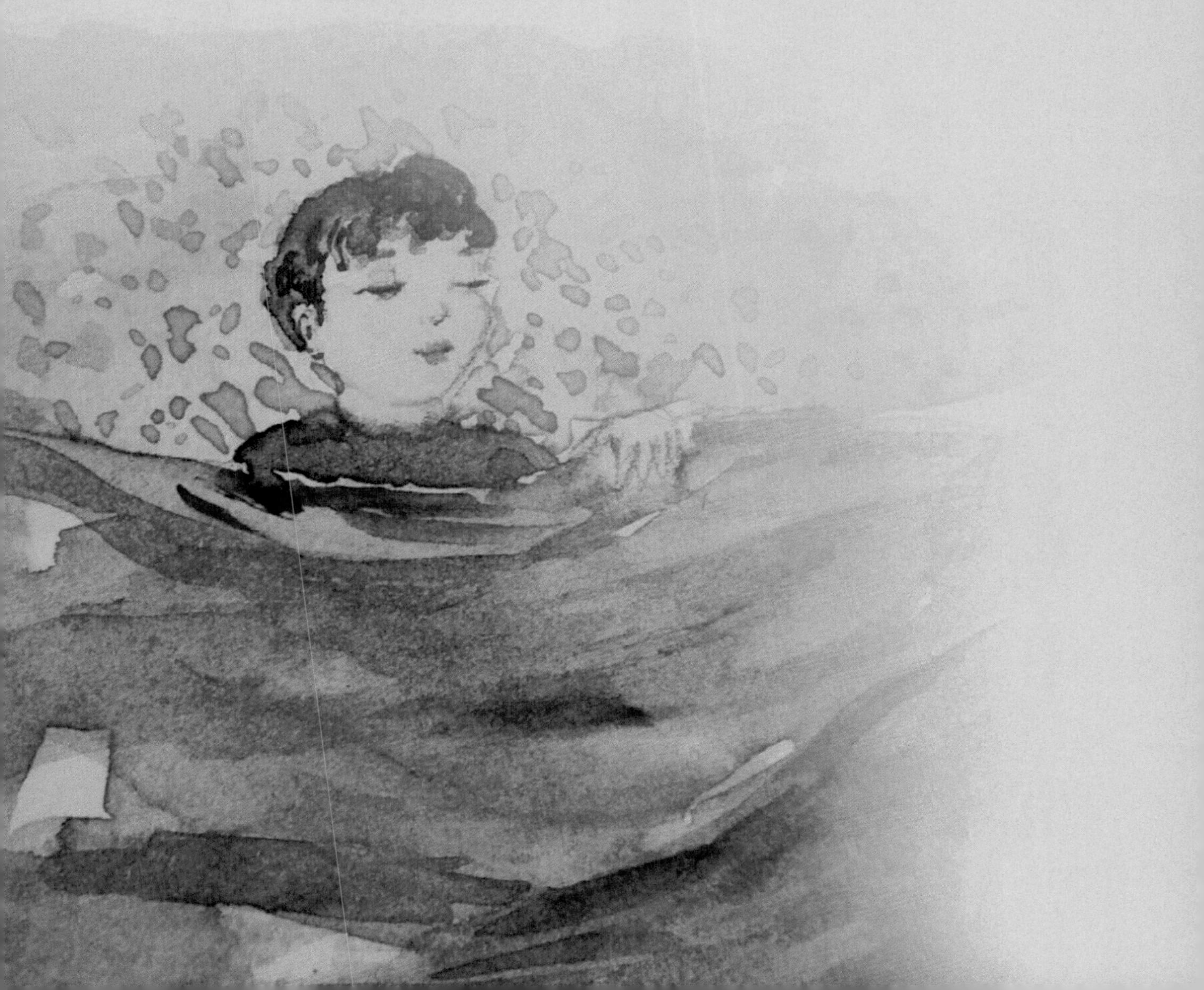

As the baby grows she discovers that her veil no longer fits.

First, her legs pop out the bottom; next, her arms stick out the sides. Hands, feet, fingers, toes—all exposed!

What once covered her body now leaves certain parts vulnerable, and unrest begins...

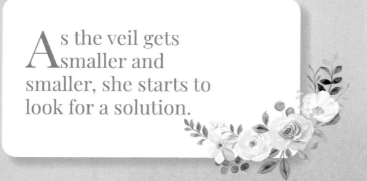

As the veil gets smaller and smaller, she starts to look for a solution.

She stretches the fabric, using all her strength to pull it end to end around her body.

She tries and tries with all her might to twist and tug and transform the fabric.

Despite her efforts, she cannot get the veil to fit, and this bothers her.

She has discovered a reality of life.

So now what is she to do?

She might use her veil to cover the parts of her that are most exposed in order to be as happy as possible with the fabric she has.

Or if she's seeking comfort, she might shelter under as much of the veil as will fit her.

While this may make her momentarily content, it may limit her throughout life. Twisting and turning as if she is in her mother's womb. Always trying to cover her body with a tiny veil that will never fit again...

She might find happiness in sharing her veil with others. Although she has less cover for herself, her heart is full of joy from giving comfort to someone else.

She can feel peace when sharing.

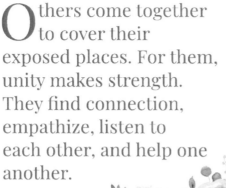

Others come together to cover their exposed places. For them, unity makes strength. They find connection, empathize, listen to each other, and help one another.

Even though some parts of their bodies are exposed, through the pleasure of acting together, their hearts are happier.

There are some who want to hunt down the happiness of others in order to be happier.

While some only think of their own happiness and are not at peace.

However, this does not mean that they want to see other people unhappy.

Greedy people can never be happy with the veil given to them. Their eyes are always on the happiness of others... that is, from the fabric they received.

They believe they will be happier by patching someone else's life into their own fabric. They believe whatever they snatch from others is profitable...

But they will never know themselves.

Their shoddy patches grow so big that they are crushed by the weight of them and still restless.

Although they may appear to be comfortable, they are not happy at all.

Some people enjoy making other people unhappy…

Envious people can never be happy because they are always restless.

Their distress makes them attack vulnerable people more and more.

In this spiral, they experience unhappiness all the time.

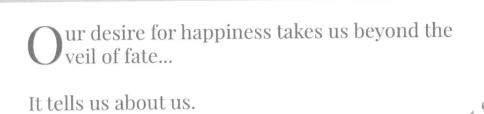

Our desire for happiness takes us beyond the veil of fate...

It tells us about us.

And just as we opened our eyes with a fabric, we all close our eyes with one. Whatever we have we leave behind.

Imagine a world where everyone uses their veil to create love, kindness, and respect. What peace that would bring us. What a fate we'd pass on to others.

Is the veil the key to happiness?

Are people the prisoners of their fate?

How, then, can one be happy?

Throughout our lives, we seek answers to these questions, either consciously or unconsciously. Everyone's purpose is to be happy.

Happiness is always as near as the first piece of fabric covering us when we were born. Our happiness is always just beyond the veil of fate.

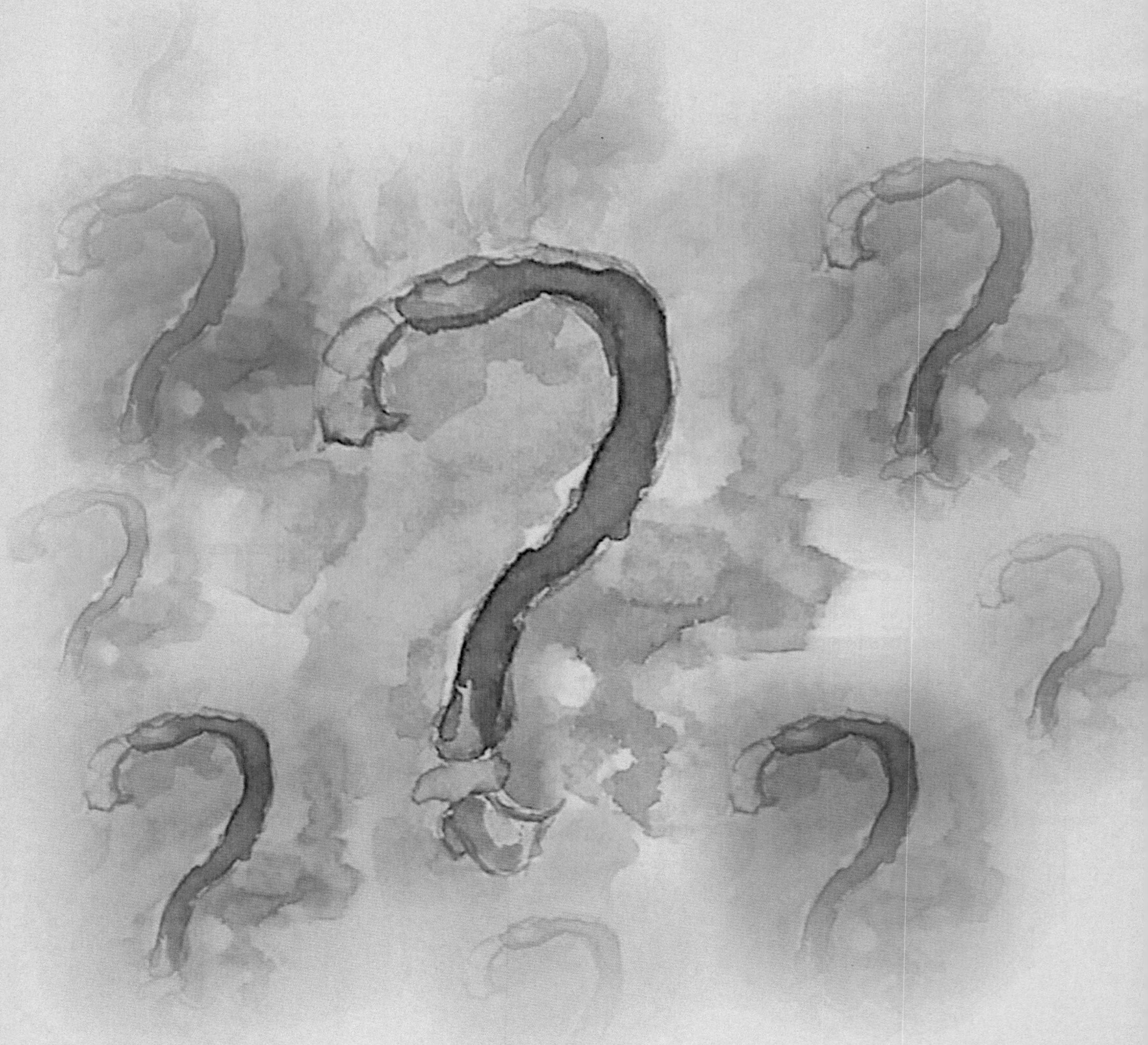

The End

Acknowledgements

Some trees bear beautiful fruits in summer when they are given fertilizer, cultivated soil, sweet rain in spring, and ample sunshine, with good care by their gardener. However, some trees grow under cold, wind, thunder—perhaps on the edge of a cliff—and bear fruit in wintertime. To some, their fruits are more special and give a different taste. Similarly, the story of this book did not emerge in an easy environment; it grew out of great problems and long-term troubles. This book is the fruit of a philosphy that addresses the issue of awareness of the meaning of life. We wish the readers' fruits to give a rare taste.

Kevin Nichols

Meet iPub Global Connection LLC

A Hybrid Boutique Publishing House and Forum for Scholars, Writers, Educators, Artists, Dreamers, Thinkers, and Survivors

With every piece of content we publish, we help someone somewhere. The company, the team, the authors, the contributors, our community, and everyone else in between—we are determined to publish our way to a better tomorrow.

It is possible!

iPub Global Connection is the brainchild of Sandi Billingslea. Originally built to showcase the distinguished academic library of works by Sandi's brother Dr. Leonard Swidler, close to a decade later, iPub Global has grown into so much more.

We spotlight voices in our community in print, digital, video, and audio formats—and we are always looking to add to the chorus. The evolution of success is found in seeing where one wants to go and then recognizing one's own ability to build unique pathways to get there. We see those builders as the future, making choices with critical clarity of mind and a love for humanity, sharing losses, embracing successes, and cheering others on, so that all the world can see, "It is possible!"

iPub Global Connection, LLC
www.iPubGlobalConnection.com
1050 West Nido Avenue
Mesa, AZ 85210
info@iPubGlobalConnection.com

Come and visit our website to stay up to date on your favorite writers and subscribe for news on new releases, events, and promotions: www.iPubGlobalConnection.com

Join the conversation
at Facebook.com/iPubCloud

Join our community
at iPubForum.com

Publisher's Acknowledgements

This book was published with special thanks to:

Jill Heins
Rob Robinson
Henry Whitney

We are grateful for your contributions.

Please show support for our authors by sharing this book with your friends and family, writing reviews everywhere books are sold, and joining our community.

www.iPubGlobalConnection.com/products/beyond-the-veil-of-fate

Made in the USA
Middletown, DE
05 July 2024

56881149R00022